To the Moon
by Sue Bright-Moore

HOUGHTON MIFFLIN HARCOURT

PHOTOGRAPHY CREDITS: COVER ©NASA; 3 (b) ©princigalli/Shutterstock; 7 (t) ©Everett Collection Inc/Alamy Images; 8 (b) ©Bettmann/Corbis; 10 (b) ©NASA; 13 (t) ©NASA; 14 (b) ©Stocktrek Images, Inc./Getty Images

Copyright © by Houghton Mifflin Harcourt Publishing Company

All rights reserved. No part of this work may be reproduced or transmitted in any form or by any means, electronic or mechanical, including photocopying or recording, or by any information storage and retrieval system, without the prior written permission of the copyright owner unless such copying is expressly permitted by federal copyright law. Requests for permission to make copies of any part of the work should be addressed to Houghton Mifflin Harcourt Publishing Company, Attn: Contracts, Copyrights, and Licensing, 9400 Southpark Center Loop, Orlando, Florida 32819-8647.

If you have received these materials as examination copies free of charge, Houghton Mifflin Harcourt Publishing Company retains title to the materials and they may not be resold. Resale of examination copies is strictly prohibited.

Possession of this publication in print format does not entitle users to convert this publication, or any portion of it, into electronic format.

Printed in Mexico

ISBN: 978-0-544-07367-8

4 5 6 7 8 9 10 0908 21 20 19 18 17 16 15

4500608016 A B C D E F G

Contents

Introduction 3
Revolving and Rotating 4
Flybys and Crash Landings 6
Blast Off!. 8
"One Giant Leap for Mankind" 10
New Adventures and Information. 12
What's Next? 14
Responding. 15
Glossary 16

Vocabulary
orbit
rotate
axis

Stretch Vocabulary
lunar
probe

Introduction

The moon has fascinated people for thousands of years. We gaze up at its glowing shape. It is the subject of stories, songs, and scientific study. *A man lives in the moon. The moon is made of cheese. The moon shines.* People used to think these statements were true. Today, we know they're not. How did we learn so much about the moon?

We started by observing and asking questions. Early people noticed the apparent changes in the moon. They watched its path across the sky at night. You can learn a lot about the moon just by looking at it with the unaided eye. You can learn even more with a telescope. In 1610, Galileo Galilei became the first person to observe the moon with a telescope. Since then, our knowledge has grown as our ways of studying the moon have become more sophisticated.

The moon's shape seems to change throughout its phases because of the movements of both the moon and Earth.

Revolving and Rotating

The sun, Earth, and the moon work and move together in a system. Let's look at how the sun and moon are related.

The sun is the largest body in our solar system. The sun is so big that about 1 million Earths would fit inside it! The sun is a star, made up of hydrogen, helium, and other gases. The gases combine deep in the sun's core to produce energy.

The moon revolves around Earth. Together with the moon, Earth revolves around the sun.

The sun's heat and light energy affect the moon's temperature and how it is lit. The sun's gravitational pull can be felt all the way to the moon and Earth.

The moon revolves around Earth. That means it moves around Earth in a path called an orbit. At the same time, Earth and the moon revolve around the sun. The pull of the sun's gravity helps keep them in a consistent orbit.

Now let's look at how Earth and the moon are related. Earth is a rock-like planet. In fact, the moon and Earth are very similar in makeup. Both are made up of rocky layers of silicon, magnesium, and iron. However, unlike the moon, Earth has a core that's partially liquid. The moon and Earth have unique surface features. From space, you see craters and valleys on the moon. On Earth's surface, you see oceans and land masses.

How do the moon and Earth interact? To understand, you need to know that each one spins, or rotates, on an axis. When it spins, only one part of its surface faces the sun. This side experiences day and an apparent journey of the sun across the sky. The other side faces away from the sun. This side experiences night. One complete spin of Earth takes 24 hours. One complete spin of the moon takes approximately 27 days.

At one time, people did not think the moon rotated. That is because the moon makes one complete rotation in about the same time it takes for it to orbit Earth. The result is that we always see the same side of the moon. We didn't really know what the other side of the moon looked like until we sent spacecraft to photograph and explore it.

Flybys and Crash Landings

It seemed like the more we studied the moon, the more questions we had. Many of these questions could not be answered from Earth. They required closer contact with the moon. The big question was whether people could travel to the moon. In the 1960s, many lunar (moon) missions sent unmanned spacecraft to study the moon from space.

Luna The space program of the former Soviet Union ran the Luna missions from 1959 to 1976. The Luna missions had the first spacecraft to impact the moon's surface. They also took the first images of the far side of the moon.

Ranger Around the same time (1961–1965), the National Aeronautics and Space Administration (NASA) of the United States launched the Ranger missions. Does it make sense to crash expensive spacecraft on purpose? That's exactly what NASA did with the Ranger crafts. They were designed to take pictures until they crashed on the moon's surface. The first six Ranger missions were not successful, but NASA did not give up. The seventh, eighth, and ninth missions were able to send close-up pictures of the moon's surface back to Earth.

Surveyor People could crash spacecraft into the moon. But how about landing safely on it? From 1966 to 1968, NASA Surveyor probes landed on the moon. They did not carry people.

In the Mercury 6 mission, John Glenn became the first American to orbit Earth.

From the Surveyor missions, NASA learned much more about the lunar surface. They took photos and gathered soil samples to help them decide whether the moon was safe for people to land on. Each probe had a TV camera to send video back to Earth. People around the world watched the Surveyor missions.

Zond The Soviets launched the Zond spacecraft from 1965 to 1970. Zond missions included several lunar flybys and orbits of the moon.

Gemini The United States was getting closer in its race to the moon. The Mercury missions resulted in the first Americans in space. The next step was the Gemini missions (1965–1966). During these exciting missions, NASA learned a lot about how to prepare astronauts for longer trips. Americans now had a new word to add to their vocabulary: *astronaut*.

Blast Off!

We learned much from the first years of space travel. But could we land a spacecraft with people on the moon? The Apollo series answered that question with a big yes!

The Apollo missions lasted from 1967 to 1972. They had four main goals:
- to design and test technology to help us explore space
- to establish the United States as a leader in space exploration
- to explore the moon
- to help people learn to work in a lunar environment

To achieve these goals, a special rocket was built. Unlike others that preceded it, the Apollo rocket had three parts. The first was the command module. It contained the instruments that helped the crew fly the spacecraft, as well as their living area. The second part was the service module. It held the propulsion and life-support systems. The final module was the lunar module. It separated from the other two modules and held two people who could land on the moon and return to orbit.

The 17 Apollo missions saw great triumphs and some heartbreaking moments as well. The Apollo 1 mission ended tragically when a fire started on the launch pad and killed the three astronauts. The nation mourned. Some people wondered if we should continue the race to the moon. After a short break, the program continued.

The goals for Apollo 8 were to practice and improve the moves needed to land a crewed module (a module with people) on the moon. NASA learned a lot during this mission. The crew became the first humans to see the far side of the moon.

Apollo 10 was designed to practice all parts of a crewed landing, except for the actual landing. The voyage was an exciting event for people around the world. TV transmissions let people at home share it with the astronauts.

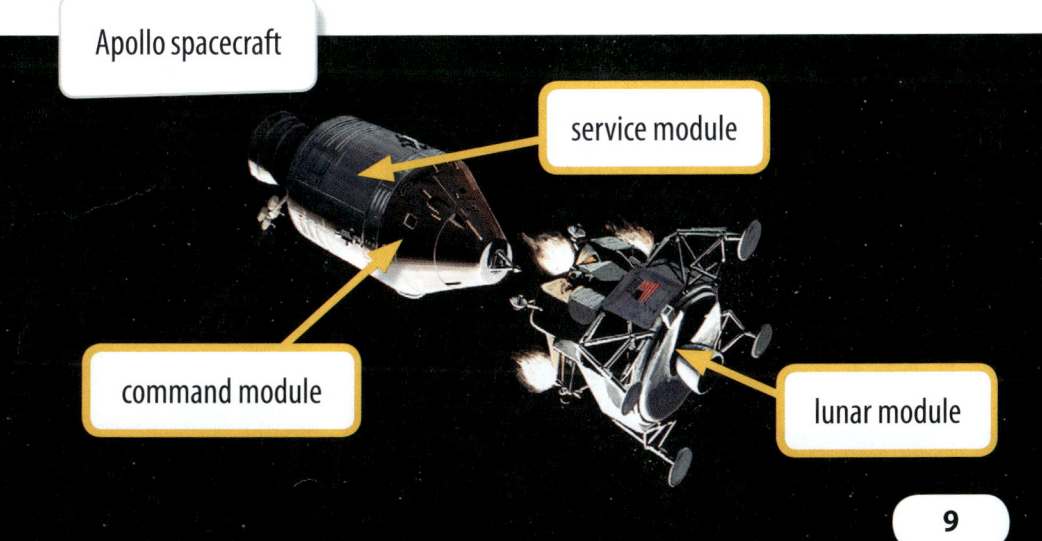

Apollo spacecraft

service module

command module

lunar module

"One Giant Leap for Mankind"

On July 16, 1969, Neil Armstrong, Michael Collins, and Edwin "Buzz" Aldrin made history in the Apollo 11 mission. Their rocket burst through Earth's atmosphere and headed for the moon.

As the rocket reached an orbit around the moon, Aldrin and Armstrong climbed into the lunar module, named *Eagle*. They got ready for it to be separated from the other two modules. Collins remained in the command module. He piloted it in orbit around the moon.

Aldrin and Armstrong separated the lunar module. Then they guided it to the surface of the moon. As they touched down, they transmitted the famous words, "The *Eagle* has landed!" Aldrin and Armstrong became the first humans to land on the moon. After all the years of preparation, they had succeeded at something that no one else had done!

Astronaut Neil Armstrong planted a flag on the moon.

Neil Armstrong opened the hatch, climbed down the ladder, and planted an American flag. With the whole world watching, he said his famous words: "That's one small step for [a] man, one giant leap for mankind."

It was truly a giant leap. Aldrin and Armstrong spent 21 hours and 36 minutes on the moon's surface. The moon has no atmosphere and less gravity than Earth. Those things meant that the astronauts could jump much higher than they could on Earth. They had space suits that helped them work. The suits kept them at the proper temperature. Gas tanks and helmets provided oxygen. Heavy boots kept them firmly on the moon's surface. Even though all that gear was bulky and heavy, Armstrong and Aldrin still got a lot of work done. They set up cameras to record information and send it back to Earth. They set up scientific equipment to study solar winds. They collected many rock and soil samples.

Then they fired up the lunar module engines and left the moon. With the three modules again connected, all three astronauts began the trip home. Hours later, the command module splashed down into the Pacific Ocean. The heroes were home.

New Adventures and Information

After five more moon landings, NASA scientists shifted their focus from the moon to Mars. In recent years, however, several U.S. space missions have provided new information about the moon.

Galileo   The main goal of the Galileo mission was to take photos of Jupiter. Because Jupiter is so far away, *Galileo* first orbited the moon. While orbiting the moon, it took many detailed photos of the moon's surface. Photography had come a long way in 25 years. The photographs were much better than the photos taken in the 1960s.

Clementine   Launched in 1994, Deep Space Program Science Experiment, known as *Clementine*, was supposed to orbit the moon and continue on to explore a nearby asteroid. Unfortunately, the spacecraft had a malfunction. It was not able to continue its study beyond the moon. But through its orbit, it was able to map most of the moon's surface. The craft contained five cameras, including an infrared camera. An infrared camera allows images to be taken in low light levels, such as those in space. The images gave scientists a better understanding of the moon's surface minerals.

Lunar Prospector In 1998, *Lunar Prospector* began orbiting the moon. Compared to the giant Apollo rockets, *Lunar Prospector* was tiny. It carried only five instruments. *Lunar Prospector* had an exciting mission. It explored the polar caps of the moon to see if they had ice. It also measured the magnetic and gravity fields. While looking for ice, it also analyzed the minerals found on the surface.

Lunar Prospector was about the size of a car.

The mission ended when the craft was guided into a planned crash at the south pole. The goal of the crash was to search for ice just below the moon's surface. No signs of water were observed.

Lunar Reconnaissance Orbiter In 2009, the Lunar Reconnaissance Orbiter mission was launched. *Lunar Reconnaissance Orbiter* mapped the moon's surface. It took images of cold places and other places where ice might be. It also photographed rough places on the surface.

What's Next?

What do we need in order to live on the moon? Could we stop on the moon on our way to other planets? These are some of the questions that people are asking now.

Today's moon research builds on earlier missions. With new technology, scientists are also trying to answer other questions. Where are some safe landing sites? What lunar resources are available? Perhaps one day, we will have a race to *live* on the moon. Maybe you will be part of the mission team!

This is one way that a lunar outpost might look in the future.

Responding

Make a Timeline
Use the Internet to research major milestones in the exploration of the moon. Make a timeline that contains each milestone date and a sentence explaining the milestone.

Write a Narrative
Imagine you are one of the first occupants of a lunar outpost. Write a journal entry explaining some of the challenges you face and what you have learned about the moon.

Glossary

axis [AK•sis] The imaginary line around which Earth rotates.

lunar [LOO•nuhr] Related to the moon.

orbit [AWR•bit] The path of one object in space around another object.

probe [PROHB] A spacecraft designed for exploration and to collect information.

rotate [ROH•tayt] To spin on an axis.